Hole In My Mouth!
- A Tallie Tale -

Written by Kristen Forderer • Illustrated by Sandra G. Anderson

Kristen is a director at an information technology consulting firm by day, but her true joy is being the mom of Allie, a thoughtful, energetic, and animated little girl. "Hole In My Mouth" is Kristen's first book, which she hopes to turn into a series about a young girl, Tallie, and her "firsts" as she experiences the world around her. Kristen was born and raised in Texas and now resides in northern California.

- -

Sandra G. Anderson is an illustrator of children's books and a lover of all things polka-dotted. When she's not creating artwork, she can be seen scouring the bookshelves in thrift stores looking for novels of Redwall to add to her collection. Sandra lives in northern California with her husband and daughter and is an active member of the Society of Children's Book Writers and Illustrators (SCBWI). You can visit her anytime at sandraandersonillustration.com.

For my Allie

My tooth is loose
so I give it a wiggle,

and to my surprise
it falls out when I giggle!

Here in my hand
my tooth looks so small,
I cradle it gently
and run down the hall.

"Look Mom and Dad!
I've been waiting so long.
My first tooth is out -
I'm so grown and so strong!"

"The Tooth Fairy will come tonight while you sleep

and she'll leave a treat that's all yours to keep!"

I wait for nighttime

then get ready for bed

with visions of the Tooth Fairy
inside my head.

I find the perfect pouch
and put my tooth in,
tuck it under my pillow
right beneath my chin.

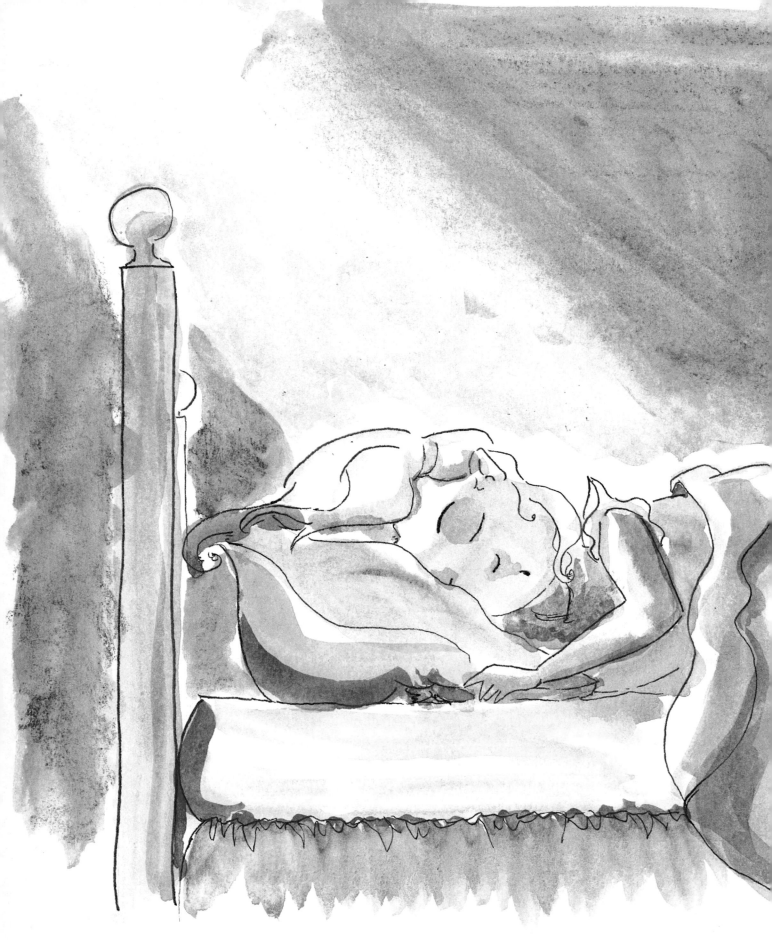

Falling asleep's not easy to do,

when the day's been exciting and the next will be too!

When the sun comes up,

though the house is still quiet,

I open my pouch
to see what's inside it!

Bright colored stickers
along with some money,

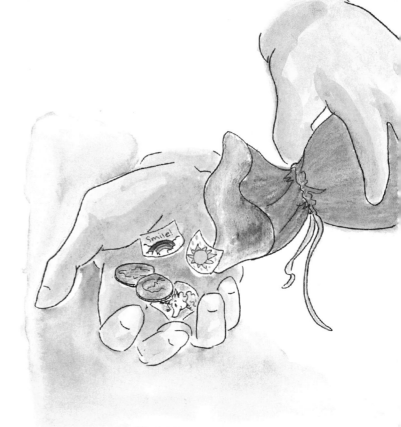

I can't help but dance
and then hop like a bunny!

I know what to expect
should another tooth fall.

This growing up thing
isn't scary at all!

Made in the USA
San Bernardino, CA
13 January 2016